For Kaitlyn and Madison

www.mascotbooks.com

From Screen Time to We Time

For more information, please contact:
Mascot Books
620 Herndon Parkway Suite 320
Herndon, VA 20170
info@mascotbooks.com

Library of Congress Control Number: 2020905340

CPSIA Code: PRT0820A
ISBN-13: 978-1-64543-300-2

Printed in the United States

From SCREEN TIME to We Time

DANIEL PARKER and **MEREDITH PARKER**

ILLUSTRATED BY
Vanessa Alexandre

Kaitlyn was an active girl who loved to play all day. You'd often find her at the park or practicing ballet.

Her favorites were the bouncy house, and swimming in the pool. With lots of friends to play with, she enjoyed each day at school.

Then one day it all changed
when she discovered a device.
It was the most astounding thing
she'd ever seen in her whole life.

There were shiny lights, loud sounds,
silly videos, and fun games.
Kaitlyn was blown away by what she saw.
She simply was amazed!

Then her dad asked, "Why don't you go outside and play?
You can't just sit around staring at that tiny screen all day."

But Kaitlyn didn't hear his words. It was like she was possessed! That device was all she wanted. She was totally obsessed.

Her mom tried a different tactic.
She knew Kaitlyn loved to cook.
She said, "Come here, honey.
Let's make a dish from this cookbook."

Before, Kaitlyn would have loved to
help. She liked making homemade pies.
But now nothing else seemed to
matter because she had zombie eyes.

Her mom and dad had no choice
but to take the device away.
That led to a meltdown—
Kaitlyn was mad the entire day.

Why couldn't she keep it?
It was the best thing she'd ever seen!
Kaitlyn asked them angrily,
"Why do you have to be so mean?"

Her dad said,
"I understand, hone
I like looking at it, to
But spending so muc
time on it is just no
good for you.

Before you know it, you're on that thing for hours at a time. Real life experiences are better for your body and your mind."

"Instead of watching videos of
things that happened in the past,
why don't you have new adventures,
and make memories that will last?

Instead of playing iPad games,
the screen inches from your face,
you can read an inspiring book
that your brain will fully embrace."

Then Kaitlyn raised a point that made her parents feel truly sad. She said, "But you use it constantly and that makes me feel really bad.

You have it at the dinner table. You have it when we play. It makes a little sound and your attention drifts away."

Her parents exchanged glances.
They knew something had to change.
Their family priorities must be
drastically rearranged.

Mom said, "Instead of using
devices to occupy our time,
let's all reconnect and use
we time to build our minds."

Kaitlyn liked her mom's idea.
Maybe we time could be fun!
Then she asked her mom and dad,
"What did you do when you were young?"

Her parents started thinking
and soon the ideas came.
Without so much device time,
there'd be time for fun and games!

The first we time was hide-and-seek,
then on to the basketball court.
Next, they baked lemon cookies,
and built a crazy, giant fort!

Each day was something different—
a new adventure they all shared.
Kaitlyn felt so special. She could see how much they cared.

Eventually, we time changed from
planned events to part of the routine,
as everyone made space
to be heard, and to be seen.

Screen time
didn't disappear
completely. There
was a time and place.
But we time was more
important—an idea they
all embraced!

Tips for Parents

- Turn off notifications and sounds on your phone. They can be distracting and interfere with connecting with your children.

- Designate "no device time" when all members of the family agree to disengage from screens and spend time together (during meals, Saturday mornings, bedtime).

- When you need to use your phone in front of your children, tell them what you are doing. ("I'm sending a text message to Daddy, letting him know we are on our way.") This helps children understand the usefulness of technology in our lives.

- When your children watch shows, watch with them and ask questions about what they are seeing.

- Listen to your children with your whole face. Make eye contact and pay full attention.

- Reflect on the role technology is playing in your own life. Be intentional with your time. Mindless scrolling has little value. Let your children, and yourself, experience boredom. When children have no external inspiration, they will create their own games. Learning to tolerate moments of calm will be a lifelong skill.

- Focus on what your child will gain from disconnecting from devices, not simply that they are losing something they enjoy. ("Let's go down the street and see if Reagan is free to play. We could show her your new bike.")

- Technology is everywhere. Resist the urge to give your children devices to be on par with other children. The skills they learn without devices will serve them better as adults.

- Refrain from using screen time to distract from strong emotions. Attempting to change or minimize a child's natural emotional experience will not allow for the emotional development they need to grow into well-adjusted adults.

Daniel and Meredith Parker are parents to two amazing girls, Kaitlyn and Madison. Meredith is a clinical psychologist at Stanford University, and has seen firsthand the consequences of reliance on devices for social connection, distraction, and immediate gratification. Daniel works as a director of accounting, where he has been alarmed by how disruptive devices have become in daily interactions at work and in life. Both are recovering screen time addicts, and hope that their story can encourage others to be mindful of the role technology plays in all our lives.